Chapter books from Henry Holt and Company:

Boo's Dinosaur
Betsy Byars, illustrated by Erik Brooks

Dragon Tooth Trouble
written and illustrated by Sarah Wilson

Fat Bat and Swoop
written and illustrated by Leo Landry

Little Horse
Betsy Byars, illustrated by David McPhail

Little Horse on His Own
Betsy Byars, illustrated by David McPhail

Maybelle in the Soup
Katie Speck, illustrated by Paul Rátz de Tagyos

Sea Surprise
written and illustrated by Leo Landry

SECOND-GRADE FRIENDS:
The Secret Lunch Special (Book 1)
No More Pumpkins (Book 2)
Peter Catalanotto and Pamela Schembri

Three Little Robbers
Christine Graham, illustrated by Susan Boase

Maybelle
in the
Soup

Katie Speck

Illustrations by Paul Rátz de Tagyos

Henry Holt and Company ☺ New York

For Erin, who laughed

—K. S.

Henry Holt and Company, LLC
Publishers since 1866
175 Fifth Avenue
New York, New York 10010
www.HenryHoltKids.com

Library of Congress Cataloging-in-Publication Data
Speck, Katie.
Maybelle in the soup / Katie Speck ; illustrations by Paul Rátz de Tagyos.—1st ed.
p. cm.
Summary: When Mr. and Mrs. Peabody invite guests to dinner,
Maybelle, the cockroach who lives under their refrigerator, ignores
the warnings of Henry the flea to be sensible and ends up
"splashing" into a big adventure.
ISBN-13: 978-0-8050-8092-6 / ISBN-10: 0-8050-8092-9
[1. Cockroaches—Fiction. 2. Insects—Fiction. 3. Curiosity—Fiction.]
I. Rátz de Tagyos, Paul, ill. II. Title.
PZ7.S741185May 2007 [Fic]—dc22 2006033444

First Edition—2007 / Designed by Amelia May Anderson
Printed in the United States of America on acid-free paper. ∞

1 3 5 7 9 10 8 6 4 2

Contents

꧁ 1 ꧂

Bug Dreams

Maybelle was a lovely, plump cockroach. She lived with Myrtle and Herbert Peabody at Number 10 Grand Street, in her own cozy little home under the refrigerator.

The Peabodys liked everything to be JUST SO. "No dust, no mess, and absolutely, positively NO BUGS!" Mrs. Peabody was fond of saying.

Maybelle was not welcome, but she was a sensible cockroach. She obeyed The Rules: *When it's light, stay out of sight*; *if you're spied, better hide*; and, most important of all, *never meet with human feet*. The Peabodys didn't know they shared their kitchen with a bug.

Maybelle was sensible, but she *loved* food. And she wanted the good stuff. "I'm tired of crumbs and spills. I want tasty leftovers on a plate."

"Don't even think about it, kiddo," said her friend Henry the Flea. Henry lived and dined on the Peabodys' cat, Ramona. "If the Peabodys see you, they'll call the Bug Man. Then you'll be in a pickle."

2

"I might like a pickle, perhaps a pickle relish or pickled pigs' feet or—"

"We can't have exactly what we want," Henry said. "The Peabodys think dogs are messy, so I have to settle for a cat. Ramona bathes all day. I'm always wet. We've got to make the best of what we have, Maybelle."

Maybelle didn't think that making the best of what she had sounded very interesting. Just once she wanted to taste food before it hit the floor.

And that is how this story begins. Because a cockroach may not get exactly what a cockroach wants, but you can't blame her for trying.

❧ 2 ❧

A Very Special Dinner

On Saturday, the Peabodys got ready for Very Important Guests. Mr. and Mrs. H. William Snodgrass were coming to dine. Everything had to be JUST SO.

Mr. Peabody set the dining room table with the best silver and china. Mrs. Peabody worked all day on a Very Special Dinner. The kitchen was full of wonderful smells.

Maybelle and Henry watched from under the refrigerator as Mrs. Peabody's dreadful big feet moved around the kitchen.

"Have you ever tasted a foot, Henry?" Maybelle thought about this sort of thing a lot.

"No way!" Henry said. "Humans may not notice a flea on their pets, but if a flea bites a foot, the Bug Man comes. I'll stick to my cat."

"I could sneak out for a little dinner before the guests arrive," Maybelle said. "I'd be very careful, Henry. I only want a teensy taste of the soup I smell. Mock turtle, Mrs. Peabody calls it."

"Mind your business, Maybelle," Henry said. "Stick to crumbs and spills."

Just then, Ramona's four furry feet appeared beside Mrs. Peabody's two big ones. "Well, there's *my* dinner," Henry said cheerfully, and off he hopped.

Maybelle sat by herself under the refrigerator and wondered, *What would it be like to eat mock turtle soup right out of a bowl?*

๑ 3 ๑

Soup's On

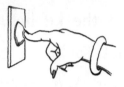

Ding-dong! At six o'clock the Peabodys'
Very Important Guests arrived.

The Peabodys were all dressed up to
greet them. Mr. Peabody was wearing a
few hairs carefully combed over his
shiny head. Mrs. Peabody was wearing
false eyelashes. They were long and
thick and made a little breeze when she
blinked. Both Peabodys were JUST SO.

Maybelle heard the H. William Snodgrasses exclaiming over the beautiful table in the dining room. She watched Mrs. Peabody's feet clomping in and out of the kitchen. She smelled the soup that sat in a bowl on the kitchen counter. And she wanted a taste.

When Mrs. Peabody went into the dining room with the salad, Maybelle couldn't be a sensible cockroach any longer. She broke the First Rule: *When it's light, stay out of sight.* She scurried out into the bright kitchen, then climbed onto the counter, crawled up the side of the china tureen, and looked down at the soup. She didn't see a turtle, but, oh, the beautiful brown broth and the lovely tomatoes and the—

At that very moment the kitchen door swung open. Mrs. Peabody hurried in. Maybelle was so startled that she lost her balance and teetered for a moment on the edge of the tureen. Then—*Plop! Splash!*—she fell into the soup!

9

ᕯ 4 ᕯ

Maybelle in the Soup

Maybelle was going to be in terrible trouble if Mrs. Peabody saw her floating in the mock turtle soup. But then she remembered the Second Rule: *If you're spied, better hide.* She took a deep breath and went under.

Maybelle held her breath while Mrs. Peabody carried the big china tureen into the dining room. She held her breath while Mrs. Peabody put the tureen in the middle of the table. She held her breath while Mrs. Peabody ladled soup into four small bowls.

"This looks quite wonderful," Mrs. Snodgrass said, sniffing daintily at her bowl. "Everything in your home really is JUST SO."

"Why, of course it is." Mrs. Peabody smiled sweetly.

Maybelle held her breath while Mrs. Snodgrass picked up her spoon, dipped it into her soup, raised it to her lips and—

Maybelle couldn't hold her breath another instant. She stood up in the spoon with a gasp and found herself nose to nose with Mrs. Snodgrass!

With a yelp, Mrs. Snodgrass tossed her spoon into the air. "*Eeeeee! Eeeeee!* A bug in my soup! Oh, *disgusting!* I might have *eaten* it!"

Maybelle sailed through the air and landed on the butter dish. A nasty human face had almost eaten her! She began scrambling around the table in a panic.

The room filled with squeals and shouts. Humans swatted at Maybelle with their napkins. The Peabodys' best plates and glasses crashed to the floor.

"It's a roach!"

"Get it!"

"Smash the bug!"

Maybelle was so frightened that she fluttered from the tablecloth onto Mr. Peabody's shiny head. "Yuck!" Mr. Peabody cried and flicked her onto the front of Mrs. Snodgrass's dress.

"Yeeeee!" Mrs. Snodgrass screeched and swatted Maybelle high into the air. The humans yipped and hopped and overturned chairs in a rush to get out of the dining room before she landed.

When they were gone, the dining room was quiet. Maybelle found herself clinging to the chandelier and looking down on what was left of the Very Special Dinner.

❧ 5 ❧

A Bug on a Rug

Maybelle had never seen such a sight—not tiny crumbs and dried spills, but great globs of tasty leftovers. Nothing was on a plate. Still, it was *almost* exactly what she wanted!

Maybelle dropped from the chandelier to the rug and rushed about trying everything—a chunk of blue cheese on a slimy lettuce leaf, a gooey lump of chopped goose liver, a smear of sweet butter with a shoe print in it.

Near the sideboard where Mrs. Peabody had put her special dessert, Maybelle found the best thing of all—whipped cream! One teeny taste and she forgot herself entirely. She plunged in all the way up to her second set of legs.

She couldn't see Ramona crouched over her. She couldn't hear Henry shout from the cat's right ear, "Look out, Maybelle!"

WHACK! Ramona's paw shot out and gave Maybelle a hard knock that sent her skidding across the rug. WHACK! Ramona sent her spinning in the other direction. Maybelle was so frightened that she could only flutter wildly. Ramona batted her one way and then the other.

"Run home! Run home!" Henry shouted.

With Ramona close behind, Maybelle ran as fast as her six legs could carry her. She scrambled across the dining room and through the kitchen. She fled to the safety of her home.

But she'd eaten too much. No · matter how she struggled, she couldn't squeeze her belly through the narrow crack under the refrigerator.

Maybelle's desperate bottom stuck out into the kitchen. Ramona grabbed it and pulled.

Maybelle fainted.

◎ 6 ◎

A Surprise for Mrs. Peabody

It was just as well that Maybelle didn't know where she was. Ramona carried the stunned bug in her sharp white teeth up the stairs and down the hall to the Peabodys' bedroom. A plump cockroach makes a fine gift.

In the bedroom, Mrs. Peabody was sitting up in bed with an ice pack on her head, weeping into a handkerchief.

"My lovely dinner party spoiled by a revolting cockroach!" she sobbed.

Mr. Peabody patted her arm. "Now, my dear. You mustn't upset yourself. Look who has come to cheer you up." Ramona stood proudly at the door with something in her mouth.

"Oh, Mama's angel! Mama's little comfort! Come to me, Precious!" Mrs. Peabody cried.

Ramona leaped up on the coverlet, put Maybelle down on her mistress's lap, and waited to hear what a very clever cat she was.

Meanwhile, Maybelle was waking from her faint. She lay on her back with her eyes squeezed shut and began gently

waving her legs in the air to see if she was dead.

Mrs. Peabody didn't have on her glasses. She leaned close to Maybelle. "What has my angel brought Mama?" She squinted and leaned closer, her nose almost touching Maybelle. Maybelle waved her legs—and Mrs. Peabody *saw*. She began to scream.

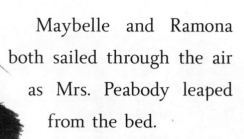

Maybelle and Ramona both sailed through the air as Mrs. Peabody leaped from the bed.

"Roaches everywhere! Do something, Herbert!" She clutched her nightgown around her and scrambled onto the top of the dressing table.

Maybelle froze on the rug at the foot of the bed, too frightened to move. Mr. Peabody began throwing things at her. Hairbrushes, pictures, and books rained down.

"Oh for heaven's sake! Just step on the thing, Herbert," Mrs. Peabody said sternly from the dressing table.

Mr. Peabody
lifted his big foot
high over Maybelle.
She'd broken the Third
Rule. She was about to
meet with human feet in
a most unfortunate way. She
was going to be squashed.

Instead she heard Mr.
Peabody shout, "Ouch, I've been
bitten! We have fleas, too!" He was
so busy scratching his ankle that
Maybelle had time to scramble under
the bed.

"This will not do!" Mr. Peabody
bellowed. "We'll call the Bug Man first
thing in the morning."

☺ 7 ☺

Henry Hatches a Plan

"Hello, Bug Man!" Henry said, joining Maybelle under the bed.

Maybelle began to cry.

"On the other hand," said Henry, "that was pretty exciting. We've had an Adventure."

"Some adventure. The Bug Man will spray us," Maybelle howled.

Henry frowned and thought for a moment. Then his tiny face cleared. "We won't be here, kiddo. Problem solved."

"Where will we be?" Maybelle sniffed.

"The Peabodys think bug spray is smelly. They'll leave for a day or two when the Bug Man comes. You hide in a suitcase tonight. In the morning you'll be off on a little vacation."

"What's a vacation?"

"Wait and see," Henry said.

"What about you?" Maybelle fretted.

"I'll be on vacation, too. Ramona goes where the Peabodys go. The Peabodys will go to a hotel. You'll like the hotel. They put chocolates on the pillows at night."

"Really? Chocolates on the pillows?" Maybelle cheered up. "You saved my life, Henry."

"Forget it," Henry said. "I've always wanted to bite a foot."

"How did it taste?" Maybelle was starting to feel hungry again.

"I would have preferred a golden retriever."

"Tell me more about the chocolates on the pillows," Maybelle said. The two friends talked late into the night, about chocolates and dogs and other tasty things.

The next morning Mrs. Peabody's suitcase was packed and ready by the front door. Arranged inside JUST SO were a skirt and blouse, a dressing gown, a makeup bag, and a pair of pink underpants with a lovely, plump cockroach hiding underneath.

ᔕ 8 ᔕ

Where's Henry?

Mrs. Peabody opened her suitcase in Room 1010 of the Grand Hotel. The Grand Hotel was even more JUST SO than the Peabodys' house—no dust, no mess, no bugs, and a sign in the lobby that said ABSOLUTELY, POSITIVELY NO GENTLEMEN WITHOUT COAT AND TIE. Maybelle and Henry were most definitely not welcome.

While the Peabodys unpacked, Maybelle crept under the bed to wait for Henry. Maybelle hadn't thought about anything but chocolate since the night before. Henry would tell her how to get it.

Maybelle waited and waited. While she waited, she listened to the voices of Mr. and Mrs. Peabody.

"I've had such a shock, Herbert," Mrs. Peabody whined. "My Very Special Dinner was ruined. And to think that there are nasty bugs in our house!"

"Not for long, my dear Myrtle. The Bug Man will take care of *that*. You can have another dinner party, a perfect one. In the meantime, we'll spend the evening right here at the Grand Hotel. We'll get just exactly what we want at the finest dining room in town. We'll forget all about bugs."

With that, the Peabodys left.

Maybelle sat alone in the dark under the bed. Was *this* the vacation that Henry had promised? Where was the chocolate? Where was Henry?

๑ 9 ๑

Under Wraps

"Hi there, kiddo!" Henry said, bounding cheerfully over the carpet.

"Henry! I thought you would never get here!"

"Sorry, Maybelle. I dozed off on Ramona. I like to nap after a good meal."

"Well, I haven't had a good meal since last night," Maybelle said, feeling grumpy. "When will the chocolate come?"

"Any time now, kiddo."

And while they watched from the darkness under the bed, a housekeeper bustled in. She smoothed the bedspread and turned down the sheets and placed a small piece of chocolate on each pillow. Then she left as quickly as she had come.

"Enjoy!" said Henry. "But watch out for Ramona."

Maybelle crept out from under the bed. There was no sign of the cat, so she climbed up the bedspread and peeked over the edge. There were chocolates on the pillows, all right. But *between* the pillows, Ramona was settled in for a catnap!

Ramona was a scary sight. But, oh, the lovely chocolates! Very slowly, Maybelle inched up the bedspread, hardly daring to breathe.

The cat snored softly as Maybelle reached the pillows. Then, with Maybelle a whisker's length away, Ramona twitched and stretched out a paw. Great hooked claws flashed in front of Maybelle's face! But the cat continued to snore.

When her heart stopped pounding, Maybelle threw herself on the chocolate. It smelled delicious. But there was something wrong—she couldn't taste it. It was wrapped!

"Wrapped!" she wailed once she was back under the bed with Henry. "You didn't tell me the chocolate was wrapped! What good is a hotel if you can't eat the chocolate?"

"I didn't know it would be wrapped," Henry said. "I never eat the stuff myself. But I'll make it up to you."

"How, Henry?" Maybelle was feeling sorry for herself.

"At hotels they have a thing called room service. Humans can stay right in their rooms and have meals brought up to them. When they're finished, they put their plates out in the hall. I've seen some things that would interest you on those plates, Maybelle."

"But won't it be dangerous in the hall? A human might see me. I might be *squashed!*"

"I'll come with you," Henry said. "I don't take chances at home, but we're on vacation. We're *supposed* to do things we wouldn't do at home. In fact," he added,

35

his legs beginning to twitch with excitement, "I saw a French poodle go into the next room. I've always wanted to try one of those!"

And so the two friends squeezed under the door of Room 1010 and into the hushed hallway of the Grand Hotel.

❧ 10 ❧

Maybelle on Wheels

Out in the hall, Maybelle saw what she'd always dreamed about—not crumbs and spills on the carpet but tasty leftovers on plates! *What a grand hotel!* Maybelle thought. She felt like a guest.

"I'm off to try some French food," Henry said. "See you back in our room before morning." And away he went to find his poodle, in great happy hops.

Maybelle hardly knew where to begin. There were plates up and down the hall. She wanted to nibble a bit from each one. Should she begin with the closest or the farthest? A cockroach on vacation has such lovely choices!

Maybelle was just about to make up her mind when she saw something that sent her heart racing: Two big shoes with a waiter in them were coming down the hall! The waiter was humming a little tune and piling all the plates on a cart.

Maybelle jumped into a green-bean casserole, and not a moment too soon. With a great clatter, the waiter picked up the plate where she hid and shoved it onto his cart. Then off he went.

Under the green beans, Maybelle wondered where she was going. How would she get back to Room 1010? Would she ever see her friend Henry again?

꧁ 11 ꧂

Eat and Be Eaten

The cart rolled and clattered along the hall, into the elevator, down to the first floor, and through a pair of swinging doors. They opened into the busiest room in the hotel—the kitchen.

This room was full of light and humans and feet. Humans tossed salads, stirred sauces, chopped vegetables, made bread. Everyone hurried.

And the noise! Spoons scraped, pots banged, blenders whirred, and the sharp blades of a garbage disposal roared in the sink.

Maybelle wanted to stay hidden under her pile of green beans—she'd tasted worse—but someone was rinsing the food on the plates into the sink.

Maybelle felt a rush of fear. The terrible mouth of the garbage disposal opened wide. *A garbage disposal was going to eat her!*

When her dish was held under the faucet, she tried to hang on to it, but she was slippery with butter from the green beans. SWOOSH! Off she went down the drain.

The drain gushed with water that pushed Maybelle toward the disposal's great, grinding teeth. If only there was some way to climb out!

Suddenly, a long celery stalk washed into the drain and stood for a moment, half in, half out. Maybelle scrambled up the stalk as fast as she could and hung on. The stalk caught in the blades of the disposal and began to spin.

ZING! Maybelle shot across the kitchen and into a blender that whirred on the counter.

BOING! She bounced onto a twirling chunk of carrot.

ZIP! She rocketed out of the blender, sailed through the air, and landed on a plate of food.

The kitchen workers were much too busy to notice Maybelle. Someone tucked parsley around her, clapped a silver lid over the plate, and sent it off to the dining room.

Safe in the dark under the lid, Maybelle was about to taste a hotel meal right off the plate in the finest dining room in town. This was more than even she had dared to want!

☙ 12 ☙

Hello Again!

Meanwhile, Mr. and Mrs. Peabody sat at a lovely table by the window, looking JUST SO. A waiter came their way, rolling a cart full of plates under silver lids. The Peabodys spread their napkins on their laps and prepared to be served.

With a flourish, the waiter took a plate from the cart and put it down in front of Mrs. Peabody. "For the lady," he said grandly, lifting the lid. "Breast of spring hen in a sauce of butter and garlic, topped with a—"

Maybelle sat on top of the hen with parsley tucked around her JUST SO. For one terrible moment, she and Mrs. Peabody looked at each other.

"COCKROACH!" Mrs. Peabody hollered and pushed away from the table so hard that her chair tipped over. She landed on her back with her legs sticking straight up in the air.

"I beg your pardon, madam," the waiter said with great dignity, addressing her shoes.

"Cockroach!" she whimpered from the floor.

"Surely not, madam. There are no bugs at the Grand Hotel."

"If my wife says that she saw a cockroach, she saw a cockroach!" Mr. Peabody growled, helping his wife to her feet. "And at these prices!"

In all the excitement, Maybelle fled to Mrs. Peabody's purse, the nearest dark place she could find. She comforted herself by sucking on a breath mint. Two human faces in two days!

Mrs. Peabody picked up her purse and let Mr. Peabody help her out of the dining room. "Bugs! Horrible bugs!" they muttered as they went.

Behind them, a room full of nervous diners scratched their ankles and checked under their lettuce leaves for insects.

Maybelle spent the rest of the night waiting for Henry in Room 1010. Henry didn't come.

☙ 13 ❧

Checkout

In the morning, the Peabodys packed their bags. Maybelle went with them to the lobby, still in Mrs. Peabody's purse. She couldn't bear going back to Number 10 Grand Street without Henry. Where was he? Not on Ramona—the cat hadn't scratched herself all night.

While Maybelle worried over Henry, Mr. Peabody gave the hotel

49

manager a piece of his mind. "Grand Hotel indeed! There are bugs in this hotel. Your waiter served my wife a cockroach in the dining room last night!" Mr. Peabody fumed.

"Impossible!" exclaimed the manager, turning red in the face.

"Not at all," said a woman holding a little white poodle. "Our precious Poopsie scratched all night. This hotel has fleas, too. Poor Poopsie is going to get a flea dip at once!"

Suddenly Maybelle remembered something Henry had said about napping after a good meal. He was asleep on the poodle. Henry was going to get a flea dip! And it was Maybelle's fault, for

not obeying The Rules or sticking with crumbs and spills.

Maybelle had to wake Henry, but she'd have to break all The Rules at once to do it. She dropped from the darkness of the purse to the floor and scurried in plain sight through a forest of human feet.

"Ack!" said Poopsie's owner, pointing at Maybelle.

"There's *another* bug!" screeched Mrs. Peabody.

"A cockroach!" roared Mr. Peabody, stamping his foot at Maybelle and missing her by an antenna.

"I'll handle this, sir!" The manager stamped both feet, one–two, one–two. Maybelle had to zigzag wildly to avoid being squashed.

Ramona was curled in Mr. Peabody's arms, her eyes wide with fear. When Maybelle scrambled up the inside of Mr. Peabody's pant leg, his eyes got wide, too, and he began jigging and shaking his leg and making odd sounds.

With a loud hiss, Ramona jumped to the floor and ran across the lobby. Poopsie the poodle went yapping after her.

"Stop, Poopsie!" her owner cried.

But Poopsie and Ramona rolled together in a yelping, spitting ball of flying fur.

Mr. Peabody reached into the fur ball and pulled Ramona out. "We came to this hotel to get away from bugs and what do we get?" he bellowed. "More bugs—and vicious dogs, too! Shame!"

The hotel manager's face was even redder than before. Off he went to call the Bug Man.

In all the confusion, Maybelle fell out of Mr. Peabody's pants and crawled back into the purse Mrs. Peabody had dropped on the floor. Now she peeked out at Ramona and waited hopefully. Sure enough, Ramona began to scratch. Henry would be going home with Maybelle after all!

The Peabodys left the lobby with their cat, their suitcases, their noses in the air, and the only two bugs in the Grand Hotel.

☙ 14 ☙

Home Sweet Home

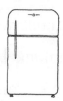

Back at Number 10 Grand Street, the Peabodys turned off the kitchen light on their way to bed.

"It's good to be home, isn't it, dear?" Mr. Peabody said.

"Yes, Herbert. It's good to be out of that awful hotel. Everything here is JUST SO again—no dust, no mess, and absolutely, positively NO BUGS!" With

a deep sigh of contentment, Mrs. Peabody followed her husband up the stairs.

In the dark kitchen, the refrigerator whirred softly. Safe and cozy in Maybelle's home, Maybelle and Henry talked about their vacation.

"The best part of a vacation is coming home, if you ask me," Maybelle said.

Henry smiled. "The poodle was nice."

"The breast of spring hen with butter and garlic was nice, too," Maybelle admitted. "But from now on I'll make the best of what I have. Crumbs and spills aren't really so bad. Anyway, we can't have exactly what we want." Maybelle said this as if she'd thought of it herself. "No more adventures, Henry."

"Suits me, kiddo."

"Of course," Maybelle said, "I might like a nice jelly omelet, or maybe a chocolate pudding with green peas and carrots on top. That would look nice in a blue bowl, don't you think, Henry? Or maybe…"

Well, even if a cockroach can't get exactly what a cockroach wants, you can't blame her for dreaming.